Other stories about Ollie and Fred:

by Anna Walker

For Nanny and Pa Wilson.

First published in hardback by Scholastic Australia in 2009
First published in hardback in Great Britain
by HarperCollins Children's Books in 2009

10 9 8 7 6 5 4 3 2 1

ISBN-13: 978-0-00-730913-9

HarperCollins Children's Books is a division
of HarperCollins Publishers Ltd.

Text and illustrations copyright © Anna Walker 2008

Visit our website at www.harpercollins.co.uk

Text handwritten by Anna Walker

Printed in Singapore

I Love Christmas

by Anna Walker

HarperCollins *Children's Books*

My name is Ollie.

I love Christmas.

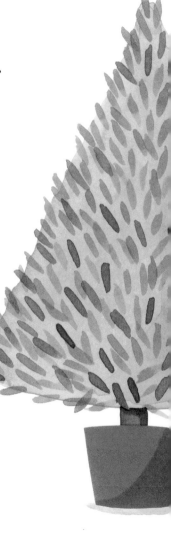

I love crinkly paper,
tinsel and string,
my Christmas reindeer
with one little wing.

I love the cow
and happy sheep,

the star, the donkey
and the baby asleep.

I love to glitter,

stick

and make,

and help bake Nanna's
Christmas cake.

I love stars in the sky,

and joyful angels

dancing by.

I love to sing about Santa—
he's coming tonight!

I love to watch the twinkly
Christmas light.

But what I love best
is to sit on my bed
and listen for Santa's
sleigh bells with Fred.

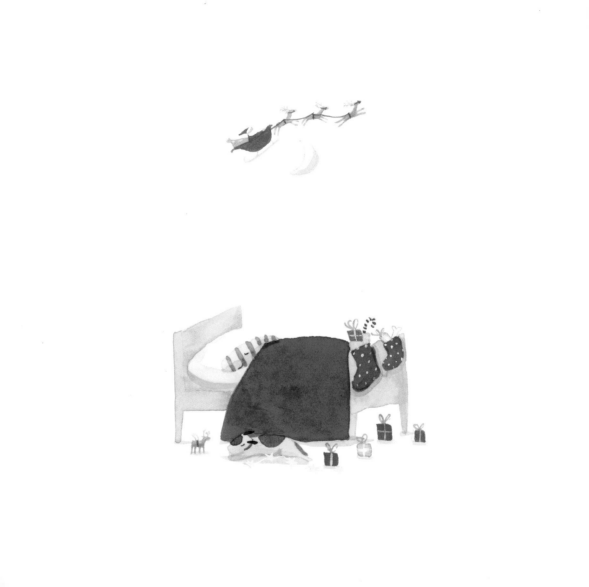